MW01539696

When Everything Changes,
Change Everything

Karen Elizabeth Russell

BALBOA.
PRESS

A DIVISION OF HAY HOUSE

Copyright © 2015 Karen Elizabeth Russell.

All rights reserved. No part of this book may be used or reproduced by any means, graphic, electronic, or mechanical, including photocopying, recording, taping or by any information storage retrieval system without the written permission of the publisher except in the case of brief quotations embodied in critical articles and reviews.

Balboa Press books may be ordered through booksellers or by contacting:

Balboa Press
A Division of Hay House
1663 Liberty Drive
Bloomington, IN 47403
www.balboapress.com.au
1 (877) 407-4847

Because of the dynamic nature of the Internet, any web addresses or links contained in this book may have changed since publication and may no longer be valid. The views expressed in this work are solely those of the author and do not necessarily reflect the views of the publisher, and the publisher hereby disclaims any responsibility for them.

The author of this book does not dispense medical advice or prescribe the use of any technique as a form of treatment for physical, emotional, or medical problems without the advice of a physician, either directly or indirectly. The intent of the author is only to offer information of a general nature to help you in your quest for emotional and spiritual well-being. In the event you use any of the information in this book for yourself, which is your constitutional right, the author and the publisher assume no responsibility for your actions.

Any people depicted in stock imagery provided by Thinkstock are models, and such images are being used for illustrative purposes only. Certain stock imagery © Thinkstock.

Print information available on the last page.

ISBN: 978-1-4525-2789-5 (sc)
ISBN: 978-1-4525-2788-8 (e)

Balboa Press rev. date: 03/02/2015

To my ever-growing family

Don't be afraid of change.
Tomorrow is calling.

Be not the slave of your own past.

Plunge into the sublime seas.

Dive deep and swim far.

So you shall come back with self-respect;

with new power; with an advanced experience

that shall explain and overlook the old.

—Ralph Waldo Emerson

Chapter One

Nothing lasts forever.

Old Ruby had lived a comfortable, satisfying life. However, everything changed the day her "lifelong" marriage disintegrated.

She staggered off into the great unknown to rebuild her life.

Her family and friends watched with mounting concern as Ruby swung precariously between despair and ecstasy. She made radical choices, some of which were potentially disastrous.

Ruby had always been a city girl. She moved to a small country town. She stopped dying her hair. She also stopped cutting her hair. The long grey tresses gave her the appearance of a green-eyed witch.

When everything changes, there is an opportunity to change everything, so Ruby flung herself willingly into the arms of an uncertain future.

She bought a small motorcycle and applied for her rider license. A year later, she traded in her bike for an old Cossack motorcycle with a sidecar attached. It bucked and weaved a little, but Ruby managed to tame it.

Her choice of abode was an abandoned wooden house that had seen better days. Ruby purchased it for land value only. It suited her perfectly. She named it Om Shanti, a Sanskrit name that invokes peace.

Grass grew through the floorboards, and the roof leaked. When it rained, Ruby placed her red enamel saucepans on the floor. She loved the sound of raindrops tinkling musically into the pots.

Red was Ruby's favourite party colour. Her feather boa was red. So was her garter. She had a red leather vest for special occasions. A special occasion didn't seem likely, but she lived in hope.

One day, Ruby found an old grandpa standing at the crossroads. He had sad eyes and a friendly smile. His name was Joe. Ruby revved her glorious motorcycle. She invited Joe for a ride in her sidecar. He said yes.

They rode towards the mountains, Joe clinging tightly to the sides of the sidecar. His grip loosened as daylight faded, and then he fell asleep.

Ruby was also feeling sleepy, so she pulled up outside an old pub. The pub looked warm and welcoming. Joe had started to snore. She shook him gently by the shoulder, and he woke with a start, staring at her wildly with vacant eyes. "Where the hell am I?" he squawked.

They booked a room for the night. There was a huge open fire burning brightly in the dining room. Ruby clapped her hands with delight.

They chatted cordially over dinner, and then Joe became depressingly glum. "Life isn't all beer and skittles, you know."

Ruby listened attentively as Joe spiralled downwards with bitter tales of unrequited love and lost opportunities. He poured out his heart until the clock struck midnight.

Ruby and Joe helped each other up the winding staircase, found their room, and collapsed in a heap on the double bed. Neither of them stirred until daybreak.

Country cafes cook bacon and eggs like nowhere else on earth. The dishevelled pair staggered across the street and found such a cafe. Wordlessly they tucked into breakfast until they were well satisfied.

Ruby leaned across the table towards Joe. "All that stuff you said last night," she began, "it's called living, Joe. It only hurts when you don't let it go."

"Bullshit!" growled Joe. "What would you know?"

Ruby held her ground. "I've been hurt too, Joe." She paused to gather her thoughts. "I tell you this: holding grudges makes you ugly. It's like drinking poison."

Joe's demeanour hardened with controlled anger.

"Is that so?" he retorted sharply.

Ruby swept the crumbs off the table with her napkin. She pushed back her chair and stood up. Their eyes were locked in silent combat. "Do you want to go home?"

"I'm in no hurry!" responded Joe. Ruby had ruffled his feathers, but she certainly wasn't boring. Besides, he hadn't done anything out of the ordinary for a very long time.

Joe heaved himself back into the sidecar. Ruby revved her beloved motorcycle into action. They headed out of town towards who knows where.

"Thank you for the bliss! Thank you for the wild unknown!" Ruby made up the words and set them to her own tune. She sang them into the visor of her helmet, and they echoed in her ears. Joe glanced at her every now and then, occasionally shaking his head.

Mesmerised by the endless vista of red dirt, paddocks, and gum trees, Ruby's powers of concentration became addled. She pulled over near a bridge and nodded towards a green patch of vegetation. "Let's rest," she said simply. Joe nodded.

They crawled through a fence with great difficulty. Ruby's arthritic hip was playing up, and Joe had a bad back. Arm in arm, they limped towards the creek and surveyed the grassy verge. At close quarters, it didn't look very inviting. They both groaned in pain as their limbs connected with the unforgiving surface. Ruby rested her head against Joe's belly and moments later drifted into deep slumber.

In spite of the hard ground, it was a long time before Ruby stirred. With a start, she realized she was alone. Her head was resting on Joe's rolled-up jacket, and the sun had slipped behind the horizon. In a panic, she struggled to her feet. Her whole body ached. Where was Joe?

She spotted him leaning over the railing of the bridge. His frame was silhouetted against the backdrop of a glorious sunset. He clicked his heels and saluted.

It was almost midnight by the time they arrived back at Ruby's place.

"Better stay the night," she said. Joe nodded.

They spent the next day sitting in the backyard, indulging in idle chatter. Ruby chattered, and Joe mainly listened.

"I wish I had a platform built high above my rooftop." Ruby sighed ecstatically. "I would write amazing novels and drink red wine with a knight in shining armour."

"Is that so?" muttered Joe.

"I could see rows of chimney pots from up there. I love watching smoke rising out of chimney pots." Ruby clasped her hands together. "Do you know what's so great about growing old, Joe?"

No response.

"We've got time on our side. Time to sit beside the fire; time to write; time to dance in the garden. Do you like growing old, Joe?"

No response.

"When are you going home, Joe?"

Joe held out his hand and caught a large raindrop. "When this shower passes."

"Oh! Is it raining?" Ruby looked skyward at the black clouds scudding above. The rain shower developed into a dramatic storm and persisted for three days.

"Your roof leaks!" Joe stared up at the rivulets of water streaming through the ceiling.

Ruby gathered up her red enamel pots and placed them strategically on the floor. "It only leaks when it rains, Joe. Besides, just listen to this marvellous raindrop symphony. *Plink, plonk, plunk!* Isn't it great?"

Joe stared at her long and hard. "You're just a young girl with wrinkles, aren't you?" They both laughed.

Ruby cooked up a big pot of spaghetti bolognaise for dinner. "I love eating spaghetti bolognaise on a night like this. It sort of goes with rain on the roof and open fires."

"I suppose it does," mumbled Joe as he sucked up a long spaghetti strand. It swirled and kicked like a worm, splashing bolognaise sauce all over his shirt. "I haven't done that since I

7

was a kid," he said with a chuckle. Ruby sponged him down with a wet cloth.

After dinner, Ruby sat at one end of the lounge and rested her feet across Joe's thighs. "Joe," she said pleadingly, "I've got these little sore spots on the bottom of my feet. Would you mind rubbing them for me?"

Joe encircled her feet with his large rough hands and gently rubbed the soles with his thumbs. "Ohhhhhh!" groaned Ruby ecstatically. "That feels so good!" Her chattering ceased. All she could manage was an occasional delirious moan.

It seemed quite natural to snuggle up in bed together each night. *Who really cares?* thought Ruby with a giggle. She particularly enjoyed wrapping herself around Joe's back. It was such a primal, comforting thing to do.

The three days passed quickly. When they awoke on the fourth morning, the sun was high in the sky. Ruby served brunch in the garden. "Will you be going home today, Joe?"

There was a long awkward silence before Joe responded. "I'd like to mend your roof first."

Ruby kissed Joe on the end of the nose. "That's very kind."

Such a clattering and banging emanated from the rooftop over the next couple of days. Joe was out of sight most of the time. He laboured under adverse conditions somewhere between the two roof peaks and adjoining chimney stack.

"Joe, what are you doing up there?" yelled Ruby towards the end of the second day.

Joe peered over the edge of the roof, grinning. "Fixing leaks!" It was almost dark when he climbed wearily down the ladder.

After dinner, Joe kept peering through the sitting room window. "What are you looking at, Joe?" Ruby was curious.

Moments passed. "Ah! There it is!" Joe took Ruby by the hand and led her outside.

A huge orange moon was rising up beyond the horizon. Joe placed his hands on Ruby's shoulders and propelled her towards the ladder. He nudged her up, rung by rung, towards the rooftop. She climbed over the edge and lay sprawled against the corrugated iron. Joe clambered up beside her.

"Crawl this way," he whispered. She crawled beside him towards the chimney stack. He pulled her to her feet, covered her eyes with his hands, and jostled her through the opening between the two roof peaks.

She felt his lips hot on her cheek. His hands gripped her shoulders. "Open your eyes!" he whispered huskily.

There, between the two roof peaks, lay a large wooden platform. "It's a castle!" explained Joe.

"Of course it is! Oh, Joe, I think I'm going to cry!" Ruby clung to the old grandpa and giggled wetly against his neck.

Joe disentangled Ruby firmly, leant down, and produced two folding chairs from beneath the frame. He also produced a small esky.

"Sit!" Ruby obeyed without question as Joe reached into the esky and, with a flourish, produced a bottle of red wine and two glasses. Ruby was mesmerized by the rich colour as it swirled into the sparkling glasses. They clinked their goblets together and drank deeply.

The bewitching moon rose above the rooftops, and a mopoke broke the silence. Joe mimicked the call of the mopoke in reply.

A rascally breeze danced around the strange couple. Their laughter echoed amongst the chimney stacks. The moon shone its magical light over all.

As they consumed the last drop of wine, the night breeze was cool upon their arms. Ruby shivered. It was time to leave their rooftop paradise. Therein lay a great challenge. Ruby couldn't even imagine how she could possibly return the way she had come. "Oh, Joe! I'm scared! What if I fall?"

Joe led poor Ruby to the edge of the roof. She peered over the edge and panicked. "No! No, I'm not ready! I've had too much to drink, and my hip is hurting. Oh dear!" She twisted onto one side and stuck her foot over the edge towards the ladder. "Oh no!" she cried again. "Oh, Joe! What will I do?"

Poor Joe tried to comfort her with encouraging words. It made no difference. "Wait here!" He backed awkwardly towards the top of the ladder, lowered his leg onto the top rung, and slowly disappeared from sight.

Ruby pushed herself away from the edge and sat hugging herself for warmth. Moments passed as she stared out over the backyard. In spite of her dilemma, she couldn't help feeling a little thrill deep inside. How marvellous! How beautiful everything looked from up here, bathed in moonlight.

Joe reappeared at the top of the ladder with a thick rug. She thankfully wrapped it around her body and felt immediate comfort. "Thank you, Joe."

"I've called for help. You'll be all right." Joe patted her foot and slid out of sight again.

The moon reflected off the corrugated iron and bewitched Ruby with its glow. There were night sounds of creaking, rustling, and the occasional mopoke. Ruby stared and stared in wonder. Her heart swelled with awe at the fullness of her life. Was there ever a woman as blessed as she?

Flashing red lights and unimaginable commotion startled her from her reverie. Something amazing was noisily happening down below, just out of her sight. A strange platform rose up above the edge of the roof, upon which loomed the outline of a huge firefighter. Ruby was immediately enchanted. If this was a dream, it felt very real. Strong arms swept her up as though she was a small child. She gazed up into the handsome young face looking down at her. Her heart fluttered. "Oh, how beautiful you are!" she cried ecstatically.

For a few moments, Ruby felt like Cinderella in a golden carriage as she and the firefighter descended slowly to the ground. It was one of Ruby's grandest moments.

The first cup of tea following high adventure is always the sweetest. Ruby and Joe clutched their mugs with reverent hands and savoured every drop before retiring wearily to Ruby's warm bed. Sleep encircled them like black velvet.

"When are you going home, Joe?" enquired Ruby over breakfast.

"After lunch. Sometime after lunch." Joe spread butter thickly on his toast.

Lunchtime came and went. Joe pulled out some weeds in the afternoon and repaired a broken drawer. He stayed for dinner. It seemed sensible to stay another night.

"Where do you live, Joe?"

"Oh, here and there. All depends!" he replied over his shoulder as he walked into the garden. Ruby watched from the kitchen window as he stooped over the garden, pulling weeds and kissing the new seedlings. *He kisses plants.* Ruby was delighted. There was something strong and honest about the curve of Joe's back. She could tell he was a good man.

Later that morning, Ruby made a pot of tea. She called Joe, but there was no answer. She looked for him behind the tool-shed. He wasn't there either. Joe had gone. He had gone home, wherever that was. Ruby was startled to remember that she didn't know where Joe lived. She drank her cup of tea alone, sadly alone.

The next day, Ruby climbed aboard her beloved motorcycle and rode to the crossroads. Joe wasn't there. She rode slowly around the town. Joe was nowhere to be seen. *Never mind,* she thought. *I'm sure he will visit me again.* Days and weeks passed. No Joe.

The summer heat was oppressive, so Ruby decided to escape the heat by visiting her three sons and families. They all lived far away, so she would need to fly from one to the other. She booked her plane fares and packed her bags. Her plan was to stay with each family for one week.

Before locking the house, Ruby wrote a large note on cardboard and pinned it to the veranda post. "I miss you, Joe. Please come back." Surely she would see him again. The taxi arrived and whisked her off to the airport.

Ruby's family had multiplied dramatically over the years. She was blessed with many grandchildren and a few great-grandchildren. The thought of spending quality time with loved ones filled her with delight.

The days and nights were filled with chatter and much laughter. She went for long walks with each of her beloved sons, catching up on all their dreams and schemes. Her grandchildren enchanted her with their optimism and vigour. She bribed them to rub her poor aching shoulders each night before she went to bed. She could feel the love of family warming her heart at every turn. How she adored these glorious beings.

Three weeks flashed by rapidly. Her eyes were filled with happy tears as she boarded the last plane home. *Home! How sweet it is!* Her home was her haven. It had a way of exuding a welcoming perfume when she entered.

Ruby was wearier than usual when the taxi dropped her off. She needed an afternoon nap. The note to Joe was still attached to the post. It was weathered and the ink had faded. No sign of Joe.

Christmas came and went. The summer heat was sapping Ruby's energy. She spent many midday hours resting quietly on her bed beside a fan. She stayed indoors as much as possible and achieved very little. Every now and then, she peered through the kitchen window, imagining that Joe was in the garden.

The constant humming of the fan began to fuel Ruby's imagination. Her fantasies ebbed and flowed with the heat of the day, and she started writing stories in her head—lots of stories. Her muse wouldn't leave her alone. It was time to start writing again. Ruby was a writer. She was born to write. It was like living with a bittersweet curse. The stories thundered in her brain until she could bear it no more. She struggled off the bed and into the study. Settling into her office chair, she flipped open the computer lid and began to write.

The words tumbled ferociously onto the thirsty screen, demanding to be seen. New ideas and inspiration flowed un-stemmed. Poor Ruby. She felt obsessed. There was so much to say. Chaos reigned in her head. The rest of summer was consumed within the haze of her literary madness.

The house hugged her like Cling Wrap. She was spending too much time indoors. She carried her computer out into the untamed garden and continued writing. Her imaginings were temporarily revived until one day when her fingers stopped tapping. She was lonely. So lonely. She couldn't write another word. Where was Joe?

Chapter Two

A writing sabbatical! That's what all the best writers did. Ruby decided to go away on a magnificent writing sabbatical. She had three good friends who lived in perfect locations. Sue lived on the coast; Gill lived in the city; and Jennifer lived in the mountains. She would ask each of them if she could use a small corner of her house to set up a writing studio. In return, she would offer to prepare each of them a gourmet dinner each evening. There was no time to waste. Ruby was restless and wanted to start as soon as possible.

It worked. Each of her friends said a resounding yes. Ruby packed her bags, boarded her trusty motorcycle, and headed to the coast.

This was her first long trip on the motorcycle. The sidecar was crammed with all the essentials: her computer, red apron, favourite cookbook, and enough clothes for each season. The sun glinted on the handlebars. Her first day on the road was perfect. Ruby sang a happy little song into her visor as she rode out of town. Children waved. She honked her horn and waved back.

The inland road lay between endless paddocks and grazing animals. Birds circled above, and she saw the occasional car. It felt so good to be her; Ruby loved being herself. She was especially pleased with herself for having made such a clever decision.

The country terrain changed as she approached the coast. There were more houses and the air felt different. She imagined she could smell salt in the air. Her heart leapt at the first sight of the ocean.

Sue greeted her with a merry jig, and the two friends squawked and squealed with delight. They spent the first day sipping lattes in a cafe, catching up on all their respective news. Ruby didn't say anything about Joe.

Ruby's coastal studio was everything she could have wished for. The little window looked out across the ocean towards a distant island. She clapped her hands in ecstasy. She could write anything and everything in such a place. She unpacked her bags, stretched her weary body, and whispered *thank you* under her breath.

Each morning, Ruby rose and did a few simple yoga stretches. Then she headed off along the boulevard for a morning walk. It set her up for the day. On the way back from her walk, she bought a few ingredients for the evening's meal. Life was good; her routine was established. She spent the rest of the day writing and resting.

Words flowed magically from Ruby's imagination. She wrote of experiences that had shaped and enriched her life. She wrote about her family and her travels. She wrote about her personal spiritual journey—her musings and awakenings.

Sometimes Ruby would walk down to the beach and stride bravely into the waves. The shock of the cold salty water always made her feel incredibly alive.

Summer slid slowly into autumn. The soft warm nights were laced with cool gentle breezes. Ah, how beautiful! Her writing became mellower.

Ruby's departure date arrived quickly. She packed her belongings into the sidecar and headed for the vibrant city.

Gill had undercover parking for Ruby's bike. She didn't ride it again throughout her stay. She and Gill chatted together enthusiastically. They had shared so much together over the years.

Ruby's city experience was everything she could have hoped for. She wrote in quirky cafes and on park benches. She walked for miles, composing masterpieces in her head. She caught buses to unknown destinations and back again. Her laptop bag accompanied her wherever she went. She wrote like a madwoman at times. At other times, she stared and stared at the milling crowds, writing just a few key sentences.

"How fortunate am I," she mused aloud. "What an extraordinary life I'm living." Happiness danced on her shoulder. At night, she slept deeply, dreaming her own stories.

There was a rhythm in the city, and Ruby was in tune. She became one with the rushing throng. She explored many cafes and historical buildings that beguiled her. The weather was often cold and blustery. Even in the city, there were autumn leaves on the streets. Ruby pulled her red woollen coat closely around her body as she scurried off to the next writing location.

Her favourite cafe had a window seat with a delightful view of the street. It was in an older part of the city, where rows of Paddington Terraces lined the footpath. Ruby's imagination carried her back to pioneer days, when the city was new.

Winter crept into the city, and Ruby knew it was time to leave for the mountains. Ruby and Gill had one last extravagant meal together. They were such good friends.

Ah, the starkness of the mountains in winter. Ruby's heart soared as she guided her gleaming motorcycle through avenues of bare-limbed trees.

Jennifer's home was perched on the edge of an escarpment looking out over a vast valley. She had generously bequeathed Ruby the upstairs attic room, which boasted the grandest view of all. Oh, the joy, the rapture! How could anyone not write a masterpiece with such a vista beyond the window?

Chilly nights and foggy mornings followed. Ruby loved the crispness of winter in the mountains. She walked before breakfast most mornings, rugged up like a polar bear. The cold air made her teeth ache when she smiled.

Breakfast was a reverent occasion. Ruby ate her porridge slowly, savouring every mouthful. She made her bed and swept the floor before dressing for the day. The colours and textures of her woollen garments pleased her. She plaited her long grey hair and draped her rainbow-coloured scarf around her neck. She was well satisfied with how she looked and felt.

Armed with her laptop, Ruby strode outside onto the footpath that led towards the little mountain village. Her heart burned with longing to write. She was fearful that her longing wouldn't translate into words.

Oh dear! She found herself hesitating at the window of a quirky antique shop. It beckoned her to enter. Should she go in? Oh, yes. She must.

Her hand trailed against the ancient timbers of a hand-hewn writing desk. She imagined great bygone writers leaning over this glorious desk, inking words of inspiration onto empty pages. The eyes of the shop owner were following her every movement. He appeared to recognize the romance that danced in her eyes. Ruby was lost in the reverie of her thoughts, imagining a time long before computers were ever dreamed of.

She hesitated and then peeped at the price tag, recoiling immediately.

"Make an offer," boomed a voice from the back of the shop. A stocky silver-haired gentleman stepped towards her.

He too laid his hands on the old desk. "It deserves a good home."

Ruby sighed. "It wouldn't fit in my sidecar," she protested. The old man's face creased into a host of laughter lines. "Indeed! Well, then, we'll just have to get it delivered for you."

Could she? Would it be insulting to make a ridiculous offer? Oh well, she would do so anyway. Ruby lowered her eyes as she indicated an amount way below the desk's actual value.

"My name is John. I accept your offer if you'll shout me to a coffee."

The colour of Ruby's face slowly changed. Her cheeks matched the colour of her name. "Okay. Really? Is now all right? Maybe we can go to the cafe over the street." She was fearful he would want a more intimate setting.

"Indeed. Why not? Shall we go?" John propelled Ruby through the shop door, locking it behind them.

The cafe was an eclectic mix of odd table settings, wall hangings, and dusty paraphernalia. The background music was hauntingly exquisite. Ruby did a clumsy little pirouette before sitting on a padded window seat. John responded with a clicking together of his heels. It reminded her of Joe.

By the time Ruby arrived back at Jennifer's place, the sun was setting. An icy blast of wind threatened to blow her off the front steps. The old desk had been delivered and was waiting for her on the veranda. It looked even more enticing than when she first saw it. Her very own writing desk, permeated with unfathomable memories from its unknown past. Ruby's heart gave a little skip.

The life of a desperate romantic has many twists and turns. Ruby always felt compelled to follow her heart. She saw romance in everything around her. Every sight, sound, and sensation captivated her. Her love of life led her forever onwards in a reverie of dance and song.

Ruby and Jennifer hauled the desk into the attic. They placed it beneath the window. As if on queue, the valley momentarily leapt into life as the last rays of sunlight kissed the distant cliff-tops. Ruby pulled up a chair and lay her head reverently on the ancient desktop. She succumbed to its mystical enchantment. She knew beyond all doubt that her muse was well pleased. Great words swelled up in her imagination, and she felt the old familiar longing to write.

"Thank you! Thank you so much," she whispered to the great unknown.

Many a woman carries Paris in her heart, and Ruby was no exception. Her writings swept her along cobbled streets and between tall grey buildings. Looking over her shoulder, she could see her own footprints in the fresh sprinkle of snow. She entered a centuries-old cafe, removed her woollen coat, and sat at a small table beside a window. The old glass in the small panes distorted her view in a most delightful way. She loved old glass. She loved snow. She loved Paris. She loved life. *Tap, tap, tap.* Ruby's fingers flashed up and down on her keyboard. Her ancient desk had become a magic flying carpet. She really felt as though she was in Paris at that very moment, gazing out at the softly falling snow. She could hear the charming French accent emanating from other customers.

In her story, Ruby produced a card from her handbag and placed it beside her coffee cup. It had a big ruby-red heart on the front of it. Her pen poised above it as she gazed again at the snow, seeking inspiration. "Dear Joe," she wrote with a flourish. The rest of the words flowed directly from her heart. She simply signed it "Love, Ruby" and sealed the envelope. On the envelope, she just wrote "Joe." The impossibility of the one-word address amused her. As she stepped out onto the footpath, a few snowflakes fell upon the three-letter name, causing the ink to run, so she wrote "snow" in brackets. She posted the letter with a prayer on her lips.

The clattering of Jennifer's shoes on the attic staircase swept Ruby back into her mountain retreat in an instant. It was late, and she had forgotten to prepare dinner for herself and Jennifer.

It was a great excuse for the two friends to dine out. Jennifer took Ruby to a nightclub, and they indulged in exotic cuisine and manic conversation. A jazz band was playing. The offbeat notes of the saxophone beguiled the two friends. They ceased chatting and rose spontaneously from their seats. Their bodies swayed and swirled in time to the music; they became oblivious to all else.

Winter raged like a savage beast. Rain, hail, and sleet pelted mercilessly against the attic window. Icy winds whistled around the house like demented spectres. Ruby huddled over her beloved desk, abandoning her senses to wild, imaginative jottings. She became pale and weak from spending too much time indoors.

The onset of spring caught her by surprise. She could smell a change in the air. The first timid blossoms shivered on a gnarled fruit tree beyond the attic window. It was time to return home.

Ruby arranged for the desk to be transported to Om Shanti. She couldn't bear to leave it behind.

Donning leathers and helmet, Ruby climbed aboard her trusty steed and left the mountains behind. The warm air enfolded her in a welcoming embrace as she sped across the plains. The scent of home was in her nostrils, and she detected a strange stirring in her heart. A tiny flame of hope flickered within her. Would she ever see Joe again?

Chapter Three

Ruby's village was bustling with life. Familiar faces beamed at her. She lifted the visor of her helmet and beamed back.

Home at last. Om Shanti looked brighter somehow. It seemed pleased to see her. The bike purred up the driveway and into the carport. Ruby clambered off and stretched her aching limbs. Growing old was a great adventure. Aches and pains were just an integral part of the grand ageing experience.

Ruby hung her helmet on the handlebars. She scanned the backyard with eager eyes. Flowers, weeds, and blossoms applauded her arrival with chaotic abandon. Then she saw it.

A crooked spiral staircase was attached to her back wall. It rose above the rooftop and disappeared out of sight over the guttering and onto the roof.

She approached the strange structure cautiously. A small wooden sign in the shape of an upward arrow was nailed to the railing. Two words were blackly inked onto the arrow: "Joe's Place."

As if in a trance, Ruby grasped the railing and began to climb. It was surprisingly sturdy, and she felt safe. There was a small landing at the top with safety railings attached. Up and over she went onto the roof.

The castle platform had been transformed into a small hut with turrets. It looked very odd indeed. A worried man with stricken face appeared at the low doorway. It was Joe.

Poor Joe. It had seemed like such a clever idea at first. Funny even. Now, as he faced Ruby, a heavy sense of foreboding seemed to descend upon him. Ruby didn't even pause to acknowledge him. She turned around and descended the stairway.

After unlocking the back door, Ruby kicked it open impatiently and hurried into her bedroom. It seemed to take forever to pull off all her leather riding gear and heavy boots.

She slipped into a flimsy black nightgown and pulled her garter up onto her thigh. On went the red leather vest; then, with a flourish, she draped the red feather boa around her shoulders.

With fluttering heart, Ruby ascended the wooden staircase again. Joe was still standing where she had left him.

Their eyes met, and Ruby watched in awe as Joe's face was transformed into a mass of mischievous smile lines. He clicked his heels and disappeared into the little castle. Ruby waited and wondered.

Moments later Joe emerged again with two sparkling glasses of red wine. He solemnly handed one to Ruby. They raised them high.

"To my lady in red!" shouted Joe to the rooftops.

There was a lot of giggling and inappropriate behaviour up on the roof that night. The townsfolk must have wondered where it was coming from. A mopoke hooted its approval.

There was no more talk of Joe going home. He was home. It was an unusual arrangement, but Ruby thrived on unusual arrangements.

It seemed that nothing could dampen their happiness. They were blissfully unaware of impending disaster.

Ruby and Joe had been out all morning on the motorbike. They had enjoyed a pub lunch and were on their way home for an afternoon nap. As they approached their little town, Joe spotted a spiral of smoke. It grew in volume and blotted out the sun. They heard sirens wailing.

There was something terribly wrong, and it was happening in their street. It was happening to their home. It was enveloped in fiercely burning flames. Ruby lapsed into a state of shock. Neighbours lead them both away. Everything happened in slow motion; nothing seemed real. They clung to each other and didn't speak. Ruby couldn't even remember where they slept that first night. Caring neighbours tended to their needs and watched over them.

The next day, they stood in front of the smouldering ruins, waiting for grief to envelop them. Joe looked so very old. His shoulders were more stooped than usual, and his face was pale and drawn. The light had gone from his eyes.

Then Ruby began to giggle. When old ladies giggle, it can be quite infectious. Giggling is usually the domain of young girls. Ruby had a young heart, so giggling came naturally.

"Joe," she said, "when everything changes, it's time to change everything." Ruby took a deep breath and then added,

"I loved living in Om Shanti, but nothing can bring it back." She squeezed his hand. "Joe, I've always wanted to live in a gypsy caravan. Now we can. Do you want to live in a gypsy caravan with me?"

Poor dear Joe. His shoulders shuddered, and he stood a little taller. "Yes, Ruby, I do."

By the time spring ended, an amazing transformation had come over the block where Ruby's house once stood. All the rubble had been cleared away. Not one but three gaudily painted caravans were encircled around a communal area in Ruby's backyard. One caravan was for Ruby, one caravan was for Joe, and the third caravan completed the circle. Curious neighbours visited frequently with words of astonishment and encouragement.

Ruby and Joe erected a hessian screen for privacy. Joe constructed an outside shower, placing an old iron bathtub underneath it. Then he built an outside kitchen. In fact, most of their living arrangements were outside. Ruby planted lots of climbing roses and vines around the sacred circle they now called home. The result was beautiful beyond imagination. Their hearts sang.

Little bursts of joy erupted spontaneously in Ruby's heart, triggered by the simplest things: the shrill cry of a storm bird, a single budding rose, the curve of Joe's back when he bent to kiss an ailing plant. She would thrust her hands into the deep pocket of her red apron and sigh with contentment. Growing older seemed to amplify her pleasure.

Ruby and Joe each had daily rituals that enhanced the quality of their lives. They both liked to walk in the mornings, heading off in different directions and meeting up at a local cafe for coffee.

They watered the garden regularly and did some weeding every now and then. Ruby loved to cook, and Joe loved to craft amazing things out of wood. They increasingly discussed the meaning of life.

Joe constructed a crude wooden table of banqueting proportions. In the garden, many meals were shared around that great table with their friends. They were such happy times.

The seasons came and went in a blur of laughter and sweet daily surprises. Sun showers, birdsong, thunderstorms, and thousands of other untold blessings injected simple wonders into the passing hours.

When weather permitted, Joe lit a fire in the brazier. They would sit beneath a canopy of stars staring at the flames. Joe liked to poke the burning logs, causing a whirling upward spiral of fire fairies. With the firelight dancing in their eyes, they often lapsed into a reverie of deep meaningful silences.

They discussed the mystery of life. They shared past regrets and sometimes cried a little. Joe had developed a quaint habit of shooting spontaneous little prayers heavenward. The passing years seemed to strengthen their connection with the great unknown.

"Are you afraid of dying, Joe?"

Joe shook his head.

"Me neither. I'm not afraid of living either." Ruby laughed loudly. "I wonder who we really are," she mused. "Oh, Joe, I feel so happy all of a sudden. I feel like dancing."

Joe rose to his feet, placed his hands on Ruby's hips, and swayed gently back and forth. Ruby hummed a little tune to assist the process. A mopoke hooted, and Joe hooted back.

Sojourns on the motorcycle and sidecar were becoming increasingly challenging. Ruby had difficulty swinging her leg over the motorcycle, and Joe struggled to lift himself out of the sidecar. They decided to go on one last day trip before selling the glorious machine.

Joe packed the most scrumptious gourmet picnic lunch. Crunchy bread rolls, soft cheese, gherkins, olives, honeyed ham, and chutney were all carefully placed in sealed containers. He included a thermos of tea and some dark chocolate. They put the picnic rug and two plump cushions in the bottom of the sidecar boot, with the picnic lunch on top.

It was a perfect day. There was a soft breeze playing in the treetops as they motored towards the river. Ruby parked beneath a huge river gum on the grassy bank. Joe positioned the picnic rug and cushions onto the springy grass. They both lowered their aching limbs into the softness.

Ruby clapped her hands gleefully as Joe laid out the gourmet meal. "Oh, Joe. I wouldn't mind at all if the clock stopped right now. I could live in this moment forever."

They ate their lunch reverently and then lay back with their heads on the cushions. Staring into the canopy of leaves above them, they succumbed to the lure of deep, blissful sleep. Little sparrows danced around them, devouring the leftover crumbs.

The following day, Ruby advertised her motorcycle for sale. Before evening, she had sold it. Joe seemed a little distressed, but Ruby appeared nonchalant. "Nothing is forever, Joe," she said comfortingly. "Besides, I've had a brilliant idea."

The brilliant idea turned out to be a dual gopher. Many of the older folk in town rode around in gophers. The time had come for Ruby and Joe to join the throng.

What fun it was to sit side by side in their gopher, puttering down the footpath to do their shopping. Joe made some modifications, of course, including a loud air horn.

He also added a canopy to protect them from the sun and rain. It was embroidered with a fine red fringe, and it perfectly matched Ruby's red feather boa. They both loved dressing up when they went into town; every shopping trip was a grand event.

As time went by, Ruby's mind became muddled and Joe increasingly suffered from angina. Community nurses began visiting them regularly. Their independence was coming to an end. The day came when they could no longer steer their gopher safely.

Ruby was blissfully unaware when Joe died. Her mind had retracted into a fuzzy fantasy land where nothing felt quite real. She was occasionally aware of gentle hands tending to her needs. Smiling angels in uniform spoke to her kindly.

Late one night, Ruby was blessed with a relapse of mental clarity. The nursing home was dimly lit. She slipped out of bed and shuffled down the hallway. Finding an exit door, she wandered into the garden. The stars were brighter than she could ever remember them. "Oh," she cried ecstatically, "they're sparkling!"

A mopoke hooted nearby. Ruby turned her head towards the sound. "Is that you, Joe?" She stumbled, and her frail body sank to the ground.

Moments later, two shooting stars streaked across the night sky. Then all was still.

Nothing lasts forever.

Manufactured by Amazon.ca
Acheson, AB

15782319R00030